MEET MY FRIENDS!
(AND ENEMIES)

STORY BY PAT CASEY & JOSH MILLER
SCREENPLAY BY PAT CASEY & JOSH MILLER AND JOHN WHITTINGTON
WRITTEN BY CHARLIE MOON

PENGUIN YOUNG READERS LICENSES
An imprint of Penguin Random House LLC, New York

First published in the United States of America by Penguin Young Readers Licenses, an imprint of Penguin Random House LLC, New York, 2022

ISBN 9780593387351   1 0 9 8 7 6 5 4 3   COMM

Hi, I'm *SONIC. SONIC THE HEDGEHOG.* I was born with *super awesome powers of speed, making me probably the fastest thing in the universe.* Not bragging or anything. *It's just the truth.*

Sonic's the name, speed's my game!

That's me when I was a little hoglet!

I was born on a different planet on the other side of the universe, so I guess you earthlings would call me an alien or a space hedgehog. Some people also call me the Blue Blur.

Something tells me they're not here to play Ping-Pong.

I live on Earth to hide from power-hungry bad guys who want my power—like these guys.

And may I say, I've made some pretty great—and not so great—friends here on Earth. Like this turtle!

This is TOM WACHOWSKI, aka Donut Lord. He's the town sheriff of Green Hills, Montana, aka the greatest place on Earth.

He takes care of everyone and everything, like people, ducks, and donuts. He's a pretty great sidekick, if I do say so myself!

He's also known as my best friend.

He's kinda cool. Sometimes.

This is *PRETZEL LADY*. Also known as Maddie, Tom's person.

She's Green Hills' best animal doctor, which means she's pretty good at taking care of animals. Like Tom.

This is DR. RO-BUTT-NIK—uh, I mean, ROBOTNIK. He's a bad dude. I call him Dr. Eggman because . . . have you seen him?

He's an evil super genius and is egg-cellent with robot tech or whatever.

But he's still too slow to catch me!

After our battle, he was stranded on the Mushroom Planet with no way of coming back. But I have a feeling we haven't seen the last of him . . .

I hate that hedgehog!

This is *AGENT STONE*. He basically does whatever Robotnik says.

The name checks out 'cause he has about as much
personality as a rock.

15

LONGCLAW *is the owl who raised me.*

16

When I was still a hoglet, she gave me the golden rings and helped me escape to Earth. I miss her a ton.

This is JOJO, Maddie's niece. Doesn't she look sweet?

She gave me the first gift I've ever gotten, which makes it the best gift ever.

This is ⓄⓏⓏⓎ. He's supposedly Tom's best animal friend, but we all know the truth.

(It's me. I'm Tom's best animal friend. Ozzy's cute, though.)

This is WADE. He's the deputy sheriff of Green Hills' police department. You didn't hear it from me, but someone (cough, Tom, cough) told me he's not the best at his job.

This is *US COMMANDER WALTERS*. Apparently, he's the dude who sent Robotnik after us. But he also gave Tom and Maddie a gift card to Olive Garden after everything was over, so your call on whether those things balance out.

23

You'll have to keep following my adventure to find out!

GOTTA GO FASTER

DORA SAVES THE ENCHANTED FOREST

adapted by Sheila Sweeny Higginson
based on the screenplay "Dora Saves King Unicornio"
written by Valerie Walsh Valdes
illustrated by Victoria Miller

Based on the TV series *Dora the Explorer™* as seen on Nick Jr.™

Turn the page
to learn with me
and my very best
buddy, Zee!

SIMON SPOTLIGHT/NICKELODEON
An imprint of Simon & Schuster Children's Publishing Division
1230 Avenue of the Americas, New York, New York 10020
New York   London   Toronto   Sydney

Hey there! I'm Moose and this is Zee
We're so glad you picked up this boo
today. We can't wait for you to find ou
what happens in this story!

The Enchanted Forest is the place to be
because all who live there are happy and fre
But when Owl gets to wear the king's crown,
he turns the whole forest upside down.
Unicornio is the forest's true king,
but he needs Dora's help to fix everything.
You can help return the true king to glory.
How, you ask? Just read the story!

Check out the last page
for a friendship activity you
can share with your friends!

In this book, you will learn to . . .

 READ with us

 MOVE with us

 **SHARE and CARE with us**

 DISCOVER with us

 **CREATE with us**

 **EXPLORE with us**

 **COUNT with us**

 MAKE MUSIC with us

Once upon a time, there was a magical land called the Enchanted Forest. King Unicornio, a kind and fair leader, ruled over the forest. All of the creatures there were free to do what they wanted to do. Honeybees could sing. Puppy dogs could try to fly. Oak trees could play hide-and-seek.

One sad day, everything changed. King Unicornio had to leave the Enchanted Forest. The kind and fair leader gave his crown to Owl and asked him to watch over the kingdom. But Owl was not kind and fair like Unicornio. He made new rules. He said that bees could not sing and dogs could not try to fly.

When Unicornio returned, Owl did not want to give the crown back. The sneaky bird led Unicornio into a trap! Owl had his mini-owls put a crack in the dam, and King Unicornio had to use his magic horn to plug the crack. If Unicornio didn't stay where he was, the Enchanted Forest would flood. So all of the creatures in the forest had to keep following Owl's unfair rules!

The creatures of the Enchanted Forest were not happy with Owl's rules. They wanted Unicornio to be their king, not Owl. They talked and talked. They knew there was only one person who could help them. Dora!

Rabbit set out from the forest to look for her. He hopped through the Fairy Tunnel. He hopped past the Elf Garden. He hopped across the Cornfield. He found Dora and Boots jumping in the fall leaves outside of Dora's house.

"¡Dora, Boots, *vengan rápido!*" Rabbit called to his friends. "I know if you come, you can save the Enchanted Forest. We've got to rescue Unicornio so he can be king again!"

"We've got to find the quickest way to the Enchanted Forest," Dora answered. "Map can help us!"

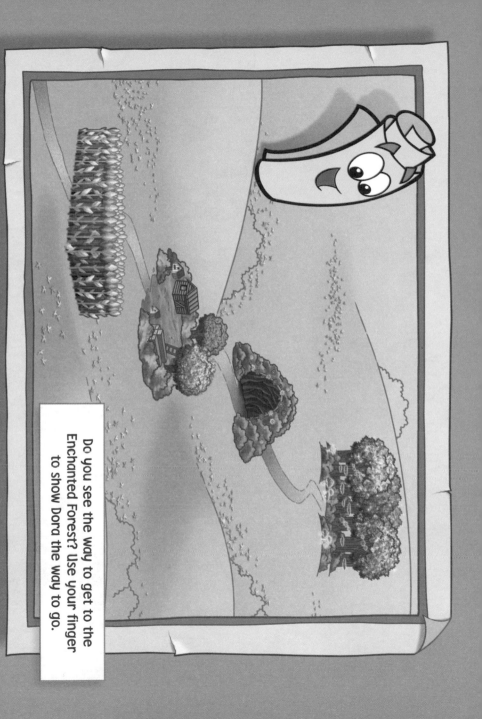

Do you see the way to get to the Enchanted Forest? Use your finger to show Dora the way to go.

Dora and Boots headed down the path to get to the Cornfield.
There they saw a scarecrow perched on his pole.

"*¡Hola, Scarecrow!*" Dora called. "Can we go through the
Cornfield, *por favor?*"

"We've got to rescue King Unicornio!"
Boots added.

Before the Scarecrow could answer, Owl
flew by.

He didn't want Dora to help Unicornio. He wanted to be king forever! He told the mini-owls to pile up lots and lots and lots of corn. Dora and Boots could not get to the Enchanted Forest.

Scarecrow was happy to help Dora and Boots find a way to clear the path.

"Owl made a new rule," Scarecrow told them. "He said that scarecrows and crows can't go into the Enchanted Forest anymore."

"That's not fair!" Dora and Boots cried.

Dora watched as Scarecrow chased away four crows that were trying to pick up corn from the pile.

"If we invite the crows down, instead of chasing them away, they could clean up the path," she said to Scarecrow.

"Okay, I'll give it a try," Scarecrow replied. Scarecrow called out "¡Bienvenidos, amigos!" to the crows. That's how you say "Welcome, friends!" in Spanish.

Dora's plan worked like a charm. The crows picked up all of the corn. They cleared the path so Dora and Boots could head to their next stop—the Elf Garden!

"*¡Vámonos, Boots!*" Dora called. "Let's go!"

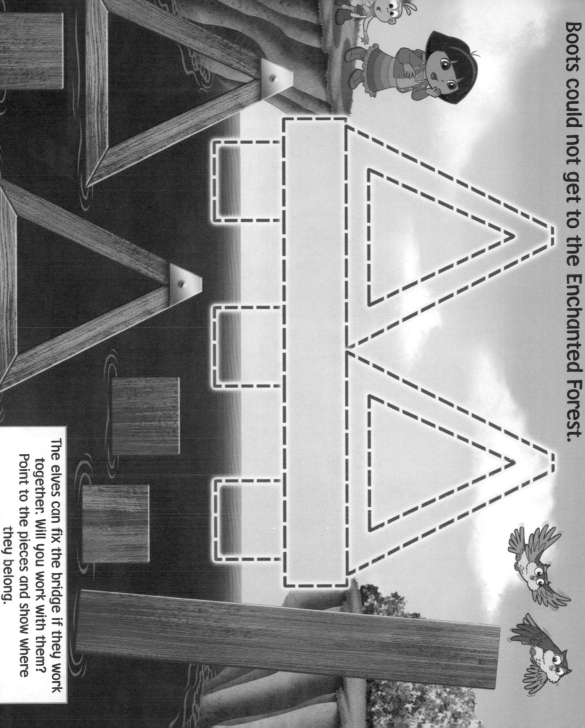

Dora and Boots raced down the path to the Elf Garden. Before they could get across the bridge that led to the garden, Owl flew by. He didn't want Dora to help Unicornio. He wanted to be king forever! He told the mini-owls to take the screws out of the bridge. Dora and Boots could not get to the Enchanted Forest.

The elves can fix the bridge if they work together. Will you work with them? Point to the pieces and show where they belong.

The elves were happy to help Dora and Boots find a way to fix the bridge.

"Owl made a new rule," the elves told them. "He said that elves can't go into the Enchanted Forest anymore."

"That's not fair!" Dora and Boots cried as they raced to the Fairy Tunnel.

Up ahead, the firefly fairies were shimmering around a patch of sunflowers. They collected light from the flowers to make their tails glow. Dora knew the fairies could use their light to show them the way through the dark tunnel.

Before they could get to the tunnel, Owl flew by. He didn't want Dora to help Unicornio. He wanted to be king forever! He told the mini-owls to blow out the fairies' lights. Dora and Boots could not get to the Enchanted Forest.

The little fairy still has her light. Will you make it grow? Rub your hands together to make more light!

The fairies were happy to help Dora and Boots find a way through the tunnel.

"Owl made a new rule," the elves told them. "He said that fairies can't go into the Enchanted Forest anymore."

"That's not fair!" Dora and Boots cried as they headed to the Enchanted Forest.

Dora and Boots were ready to rescue King Unicornio. They had made it across the Cornfield, past the Elf Garden, and through the Fairy Tunnel. There was just one thing left for them to do. They had to open the magic door that led to the Enchanted Forest.

Can you say the magic words to open the door? *¡Puerta mágica!* That means "magic door." Say *"¡Puerta mágica!"*

After they crossed through the magic door, Dora and Boots were sad to see how much the Enchanted Forest had changed. There were no scarecrows in the forest. There were no elves in the forest. There were no fairies in the forest. Owl even told the squirrels that they weren't allowed in the Enchanted Forest anymore! Rabbit came hopping over to Dora and Boots.

"I'll take you to Unicornio, quick," he whispered to them. "He's protecting the forest with his horn."

"We've got to help him!" Dora agreed as she followed Rabbit. Before they could get to the dam, Owl flew by. He didn't want Dora to help Unicornio. He wanted to be king forever! He told the mini-owls to make more leaks. Dora and Boots had to stay to plug the dam too!

Dora looked over at the kind and fair Unicornio. He was so brave and loyal. He was not just a great leader, he was a good friend, too.

"Good friends, that's it!" Dora cried. "We made lots of friends today. Maybe they can help us one more time."

Dora and Boots thought about the friends they met on their way to the Enchanted Forest. The elves were really good at fixing things, so Dora sent Rabbit to go get them.

"Tell the elves to bring their tools!" she called to Rabbit as he hopped away. "¡Rapido!"

Quick as a flash, the elves came with their tools. They were eager to help fix the dam so that Unicornio could return to the Enchanted Forest.

Once the dam was all fixed up, it was time for the friends to head back into the Enchanted Forest and get Unicornio's crown back.

All of the creatures wanted Owl to leave the forest. But that was not fair either. The Enchanted Forest was for everyone!

"Owl, you are very smart, but you must learn to get along with others and treat everyone fairly," Unicornio told him. "I want you to do a service for everyone in the forest."

Owl was told to invite everyone to the biggest party the Enchanted Forest has ever seen. Then Owl returned the crown to King Unicornio. All of the creatures celebrated King Unicornio's return to the throne. They danced and sang as fireworks flashed in the sky.

¡Viva el rey Unicornio! Long live King Unicornio!

Dear parents,

We hope your child enjoyed this enchanted Dora adventure. To extend this story, have a conversation with your child about it. You can ask who her favorite friend was in the Enchanted Forest and why, or have her tell you why Unicornio was a better king than Owl.

This book is also a great starting point for talking to your child about the importance of caring and sharing. Remind her that everyone pitched in and helped Dora when she couldn't finish a task alone. It's important to share and care with our friends every day. Here's a friendship activity your child will enjoy playing with her friends.

Picture This!

Give your child and her best friend construction paper and crayons.

Tell them each to draw a picture of something they love to do together. You can help them by talking about things they enjoy doing such as playing sports, going to the movies, riding their bicycles, etc.

Don't let them see each other's drawings before they are done!

When they are finished, have them exchange their drawings! Your child will love sharing a picture she drew herself with her best friend and also receiving a picture her friend drew especially for her.

From your friends at Nickelodeon and Simon Spotlight